The Perfect Kitten

Other titles by Holly Webb

The Hounds of Penhallow Hall:

Winter Stories:

Animal Stories:

The Perfect Kitten

Holly Webb
Illustrated by Sophy Williams

stripes

For all the brave, loving people who adopt an animal
that isn't "perfect"

STRIPES PUBLISHING LIMITED
An imprint of the Little Tiger Group
1 Coda Studios, 189 Munster Road,
London SW6 6AW

A paperback original
First published in Great Britain in 2019

Text copyright © Holly Webb, 2019
Illustrations copyright © Sophy Williams, 2019
Author photograph copyright © Charlotte Knee Photography

ISBN: 978-1-78895-017-6

A CIP catalogue record for this book is available from the British Library.

Printed and bound in the UK.

The Forest Stewardship Council® (FSC®) is a global, not-for-profit
organization dedicated to the promotion of responsible forest management
worldwide. FSC defines standards based on agreed principles for responsible
forest stewardship that are supported by environmental, social, and economic
stakeholders. To learn more, visit www.fsc.org

10 9 8 7 6 5 4 3 2

Chapter One

Abi stared at her mum and stepdad, her mouth hanging open. The cereal and milk slid off her spoon and Ruby giggled. "Look what you're doing!" she said.

"Do you really mean it?" Abi asked her mum. "You're not joking?"

Her mum and stepdad grinned at each other.

"Of course we mean it," Abi's mum said. "We're absolutely serious!"

"Oooh, your milk's going everywhere," Ruby said, and Abi quickly put the spoon back in her bowl.

"Didn't you hear what Mum just said?" she asked her little sister, and when Ruby looked confused she told her, "We can get a cat!"

"Today?" said Ruby hopefully. Ruby was only four and she didn't like waiting for things to happen.

Abi looked doubtfully at her mum

and stepdad. She had a feeling that getting a cat would take a while, especially if they were going to an animal shelter to find one.

"No, Ruby, not today," Chris, Abi's stepdad, said gently. "But we can have a look at photos of the cats we might get, on the computer. There's an animal shelter not far from here, Linfield Cats and Dogs. They put photos of the animals that need homes on their website."

"I want a cat *now*." Ruby sighed and her nose wrinkled the way it did when she was about to get upset.

"If you finish up your breakfast, we could look at the pictures now," Mum suggested, and Ruby nodded and started to eat her cereal very fast.

Abi looked at her bowl – she'd almost finished anyway and she was too excited to eat any more. She'd been trying to persuade her mum and Chris that they should get a cat for ages. They'd always said Ruby was too little and she might chase a cat or try to push it around in her toy pushchair. Abi had tried telling them she'd watch Ruby like a hawk and make sure she didn't do anything so silly, but they'd always said no – until today.

"Are there lots of cats on the website?" she asked, and Chris nodded.

"Yes! I had a quick look yesterday. There were loads."

"Oh wow…" Abi murmured, clenching her fingers into her palms. She wanted to bounce up from the table and look at the photos straight away. What sort of cats would there be? she wondered. And what cat would she like, if she had a choice?

Black cats were beautiful and mysterious, and she loved it when they had little white paws. Or maybe they could get a tabby – all those gorgeous stripes. Then again, what about a tortoiseshell? Her friend Sky from school had a tortoiseshell called Wanda who was white with ginger and black splashes, and one ginger ear and one black ear. Even her whiskers were white on one side and black on the other. Wanda was the cutest cat Abi had ever seen.

In the end, Abi decided she didn't mind. A cat of their own would be wonderful whatever colour it was, as long as it was friendly and didn't mind being stroked. Maybe it would even sleep on her bed, or take turns between her bed and Ruby's.

"Have you nearly finished?" she asked Ruby hopefully. She watched as her sister chased the last Rice Krispies round her bowl. As soon as she had finished, Abi jumped up eagerly.

"Let's all go and sit on the sofa," Mum suggested. "Chris, if you bring your laptop over, we can look at the cats together."

Abi's stepdad went to fetch the computer and they all snuggled up on the sofa. Ruby climbed on to Abi's lap and Abi peered round her at the screen.

"Are you all right like that?" Mum asked doubtfully, and Abi nodded. She was a bit squished, but she didn't mind as Ruby was so cuddly. Soon it might be Ruby *and* a cat sitting on her!

"Oh, look…" Abi whispered, and Ruby reached out to pat the screen. Staring out at them was a black cat with round green eyes, like marbles.

"She's called Meg," Chris said. "What a beauty."

"I want that cat," Ruby announced.

"She's lovely," Mum agreed. "But don't you think we should look at *all* the cats before we decide? And I'm afraid it says Meg needs a home without young children because she's a bit nervous."

Abi sighed but she understood why they couldn't adopt Meg. A nervous cat probably wasn't going to enjoy being loved by Ruby. They needed a super friendly cat. "Let's look at some more, Ruby. Oh wow, kittens!"

"Kittens!" Ruby and Mum echoed together, and Chris laughed. "They're very cute!"

The black kittens were curled up together in a basket, staring up at the camera. They looked surprised, as if the flash had woken them up.

"Aren't they fluffy?" Abi said. She hadn't even thought about getting a long-haired cat. This was so exciting! "I'm not sure how we'll ever choose…" she said to Mum. "I want all of them."

"I know." Her mum laughed. "Once we've registered with the shelter, they'll come over for a home visit to check we're suitable. Maybe they can suggest some cats that will be just right for us." Then she shook her head. "I should have said that the other way round. Some cats that *we'll* be just right for!"

Abi nodded and smiled. It was the nicest thought. There was a gorgeous cat waiting for them at the shelter and they would be the perfect home for it.

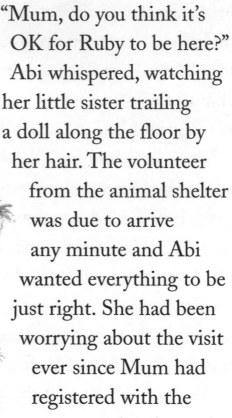

"Mum, do you think it's OK for Ruby to be here?" Abi whispered, watching her little sister trailing a doll along the floor by her hair. The volunteer from the animal shelter was due to arrive any minute and Abi wanted everything to be just right. She had been worrying about the visit ever since Mum had registered with the shelter the previous weekend.

"What do you mean?" Mum gave her a confused look.

"Just … maybe Chris could take her to the park? Or the shops? What if the people from the shelter think she's too little to have a cat?" Ruby had been so excited all week but there was a chance that she might come across as really silly…

Mum smiled at her. "It's OK, Abi. We said we're interested in rehoming a cat that would be happy around a younger child, so we don't need to pretend we don't have Ruby. And we want to get a cat that will actually *like* living here. I think children aged nine and four should be fine for most cats."

"Yes … we tidied up though," Abi pointed out. "To make us look like better cat owners. Isn't that the same thing?"

"No, it isn't!" Mum looked around at the unusually tidy kitchen. "But I know what you mean. I don't think cats care about mess. It's the people from the shelter I was tidying up for."

"They're here!" Abi jumped as the bell rang and Ruby rushed to answer it. Luckily Chris got there first, and then Ruby went suddenly shy as she saw a strange woman on the doorstep and hid behind his legs.

"Hi! Come in – would you like some tea?" Mum asked.

But the woman – the name badge on her fleece said Maria – didn't come any further in, even though Chris was holding the door open for her. She was standing just inside the gate, watching the road and looking rather worried. Then she turned to them and smiled anxiously.

"Look, I'm really sorry…" she started to say and then glanced down at her feet as though she didn't know quite how to go on. "It's our fault. I should have realized before I came out to see you… I didn't check the address."

"What is it?" Chris asked, frowning. "Is there a problem?"

Abi slipped her hand into Mum's.

She wasn't sure what was going on, but she could tell it wasn't good.

"It's your road," Maria explained. "It's so busy, you see. There are a few main roads through town that are a problem and this is one of them. We rehomed a cat near here last year and she was hit by a car. After that we decided we wouldn't let anyone along this road take one of our cats. It's just too dangerous."

"I don't think our road's that busy," Abi said stubbornly to Mum. Chris had taken Ruby out to buy some bread for lunch but it was mostly to give them something to do. Ruby didn't understand why Maria hadn't stayed to look around the house or why they weren't getting a cat now, and she kept asking about it.

"I suppose we're used to the road." Mum sighed. "I didn't think it was busy either, until she said. But she's right."

"Cats are clever though – I bet it would be OK. Couldn't we just go to another shelter and see if the people there don't mind about the road?"

"We *could*… But remember what Maria said about it being really difficult for cats to judge how fast cars are going, especially in the evening when it's getting dark. That's when they're most likely to get hurt." Mum turned round and gave Abi a hug.

"I know it doesn't seem fair, I'm sad about it too. But what if we did get a cat and we all fell in love with her and then she was hurt? Wouldn't that be worse than not having a cat at all?"

"No," Abi said crossly. She knew Mum was right, really – but it didn't mean she had to like it.

Chapter Two

"When are you getting your cat?"
Sky asked, grabbing at Abi's hands.
She had dashed over to Abi as soon as
she saw her come into the playground,
wanting to hear her cat news. Abi
had told Sky they were having a visit
from the shelter and she was almost
as excited about Abi getting a cat as
Abi was.

Abi made a face. "We aren't. The shelter said our road's too busy – they can't let us have one."

Sky stared at her. "No! I didn't even know they could do that. What did your mum and Chris say?"

"That the shelter is right." Abi sighed. "And I know they are, really, but I was so happy, thinking we were going to have a cat at last. You're so lucky to live on a quiet road."

"I've never even thought about it," Sky said. "Wanda goes out all the time. But there are people on your road who have cats, aren't there?"

"Yeah. I suppose their cats are just really careful. And they haven't come from shelters." Abi slumped down on a bench. "I was so excited…"

22

"It doesn't seem fair." Sky sat down and put her arm round Abi's shoulders. "You'd be such a good cat owner, Wanda loves it when you come over."

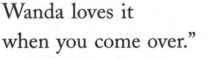

"Mum suggested we get some fish." Abi shook her head. "It just isn't the same thing."

"You can't stroke a fish," Sky agreed. "What about a dog?"

"Nope. Mum thinks we're all

too busy to manage the walks and everything. And I like dogs, but not the same way that I love cats." She giggled. "Chris said maybe we should get a lizard and Ruby thought that was a great idea. I've never seen Mum look so worried." Then her smile faded and she looked miserably at Sky. "I don't see how we can ever get a cat, not unless we move house."

"Look at these – oh, little sweethearts!" Maria peered into the box. "They're tiny. Maybe six weeks, do you think? They're early, we haven't hit kitten season yet!"

The three kittens peered back up at

her cautiously, eyes round and wary. There was nothing else in the box with them, not even an old towel, and they were huddled close together. Their mother was gone and they were cold and scared.

"Where did they come from?" Lily asked, coming to look. "Wow, they *are* pretty. Gorgeous stripey tabbies – and we don't often get a pure white kitten."

Maria picked up the white kitten gently. "She's a girl. Isn't she lovely? And what blue eyes! They were left behind the wheelie bins outside the supermarket. One of the workers from the warehouse brought them in. He said he wished he could keep them but he didn't think they'd like his dog."

"At least they weren't dumped until they started eating solid food," Lily said. "Poor little loves – they look really lost." Then she laughed as the white kitten let out a loud, squeaky mew. "Was that because I mentioned food? Are you hungry?" She tickled her under the chin and the white kitten gazed at her in surprise and then mewed again. "Let's get you three into a pen and then we can try you on a little bit of wet food. They don't look too skinny, do they? Someone must have been looking after their mum pretty well. I guess they just didn't want the kittens."

The white kitten wriggled and squealed, struggling to get back to her brother and sister. She wanted her mother more, but the other kittens were the only thing that she knew in this strange place. They would have to do.

"Yes, it's OK, here you go." Maria slipped her back into the box with the others. "We'll put the box in the pen with them for the time being, shall we? It might help them feel safe."

The white kitten huddled gratefully

with the others, letting them nuzzle her all over. Then the three kittens froze as the box was picked up again. They skidded a little on the cardboard, sinking in their tiny claws and mewing in panic. What was happening? Where were they going now?

"Do you think they're big enough to get out, or shall we tip the box on its side?" Maria asked.

"Mmmm. Tip it over, I'd say. It will take them ages to climb out and they might not be able to get back in again. A box isn't much comfort, but it's all they've got at the minute."

Lily reached in and gathered up the kittens in a furry, squeaking mass until Maria had turned the box on to its side, so the kittens could easily step out into their pen. "There! Now you can have a little look around."

The two tabby kittens looked at the open side of the box, and then padded slowly towards it. They peered out and snuffled at the air, then they set off to explore the pen. The white kitten watched them but she took a while to follow. The box felt safe and she didn't like the bright lights.

But she didn't like being left alone either, and at last she stepped out of the box and began to sniff her way around.

She was in the back of the pen, padding her paws on the soft basket, when she smelled food. She hadn't noticed the dish being put into the pen and she dashed over to join the other kittens. Her tabby sister was actually standing in the food bowl. The white kitten had to eat around her but she was so hungry that she didn't care.

"Did you see that?" Maria crouched down by the pen to watch the three kittens eating. "She took ages to notice the food. The other two heard me opening the door and they rushed straight up. The white one just kept looking at the basket."

"Maybe she wasn't as hungry?" Lily suggested, but then she shook her head. "No, look at her now, she's eating like she's half-starved."

"Yeah…" Maria clicked her fingers and the two tabby kittens looked up at once, their ears twitching. It was obvious they'd heard her. When she didn't do anything else, they went back to eating as fast as they could.

The white kitten didn't look up.

"I suppose we should have guessed that she might be deaf," Lily said, looking at the white kitten. "White cats quite often are, and I've heard that if they have blue eyes it's even more likely. Poor little thing."

"It doesn't seem to bother her though," Maria pointed out. "She's just as big as the other two, so it hasn't stopped her feeding."

Lily nodded. "But it's going to make it harder to find her a home."

The white kitten licked around her bit of the food dish, and then licked her tabby sister's paws too. She sat down by the bowl and yawned, showing tiny needle-sharp teeth.

Then she looked over at the cat bed and stood up slowly. Her stomach looked a lot rounder than it had ten minutes before and she rolled a little from side to side as she stomped across the pen. The two tabby kittens gave the empty dish a last clean and then followed her, clambering into the squashy cat bed and slumping down together before falling asleep in seconds.

"Maybe it won't be so difficult to rehome her," Maria said, smiling. "She's so sweet – they all are – but the blue eyes make her a bit special. And it isn't all that hard to have an indoor cat. We just need to find the right person." Then she looked thoughtful. "Actually, I might have an idea…"

Chapter Three

"Hang on a minute, Abi, that's my phone ringing." Mum put down Abi's homework book and ferreted under Ruby's pile of drawings for her mobile.

Abi went back to frowning at her literacy task and chewing her pencil, but after a moment or two she looked up and started to listen carefully to Mum's end of the phone call.

"Oh yes, we'd definitely be interested. Yes, I do see that it's harder if she can't go out and I'll have to talk it over with my husband, but we'd love to have a look."

"I drew a cat!" Ruby announced, holding up her picture to show Abi.

"Nice! Shh a minute, Ruby, I want to hear what Mum's saying."

"Yes, I think we could come tomorrow. Is about half past four OK? I'm a teacher, you see. I can't usually get back from school before then."

Chris wandered into the kitchen and opened the fridge to get the ingredients for dinner. "Who's your mum talking to?" he whispered to Abi as he pulled out a bag of vegetables.

"I don't know! But we're going

somewhere. And … and it sounds like it might be about a cat…" Abi grabbed his hand and squeezed it tight, staring at Mum hopefully as she ended the call.

"You guessed who that was then," she said, looking happily at Abi. "I can tell from your face!"

"Was it the shelter?" Abi gasped. "Have they changed their mind? Can we have a cat?"

"Yes! Well, maybe. Me and Chris need to talk about it first." She glanced at him. "They've got a kitten – a lovely little white one. But she's deaf, completely deaf, they think. She'd need to live indoors because she'd never be safe anywhere near a road. So … that was them ringing to ask if we'd like to have an indoor kitten."

"An indoor kitten!" Abi breathed. "A white kitten? To be ours?"

"A kitten!" Ruby bounced up and down on her chair and banged a handful of pencils on the table. "A kitten!"

Chris laughed. "At least it wouldn't matter that Ruby's noisy, I suppose. I don't know – how do you keep a cat indoors? I've never even thought about it."

"They said they'd make sure we know everything we'd need to, but we have to understand it's a big commitment," Mum said, looking seriously at Abi and Ruby. "I suppose we'd have to be really careful about opening the doors."

"And keeping the windows closed," Abi suggested.

"Yes…" Chris put the pan on the hob and reached for the oil. "We could do that, though, couldn't we?"

"Let's see what they say." Mum glanced at Abi. "Try not to get too excited, darling. It sounds wonderful, but we need to know if we can look after an indoor kitten before we say yes."

"We can go and see her though? And find out?" Abi looked hopefully from her mum to Chris and back again, and they nodded. Her mum was smiling.

They might really be able to have a kitten, after all…

Maria led the way along a corridor lined with cat pens. Abi hadn't thought there would be so many. They were almost all full too. Cats and kittens were lounging in baskets or standing by the wire doors looking back at her.

"Here we are," Maria said, smiling at Abi and Ruby, who was hanging on to Mum's hand and dancing up and down. "This is the white kitten we'd like you to meet."

Abi looked through the door of the pen. There were three kittens in there. Two were tabbies who were rolling around on the floor playing with a toy mouse with a long string tail. The third was a white kitten who was lying in the basket and watching the others. She looked very grand compared to the scrapping tabbies, almost regal, Abi thought.

"She's beautiful," Mum said, sounding a bit surprised.

"Isn't she?" Maria agreed. "And she's very friendly. We've only had them for a couple of days, but she's settled in really well. She loves being stroked." She looked at Abi's mum and Chris hopefully. "So if it's OK with you, I'll bring her to one of our meeting rooms and we can have a chat about how to take care of a deaf cat."

"That would be great," Chris said. "We'd really like to know more about what we'd need to do. I've been thinking about it ever since you phoned, and so have the girls. If we can look after an indoor cat, it wouldn't matter that we live on such a busy road."

"Exactly." Maria nodded. "Another

thing that made us think of you was your registration form. We saw that Chris works from home. Indoor cats need to have someone around for company, you see."

Chris looked pleased. "Yeah, I suppose that makes sense."

Maria nodded. "OK, if you go along to that room at the end there, I'll bring her through."

"Has she got a name?" Abi asked suddenly, looking back from the door of the cat meeting room.

Maria shook her head. "Not yet. They've only just come in and we haven't decided on anything yet." She smiled. "So if you adopt her, maybe you could name her."

What would be a good name for a

white cat? Abi wondered as she waited, perched excitedly on the edge of a chair. Snowball and Snowdrop were really cute but it would be nice to have something a bit different. Lots of white cats were called Snowball. She looked round hopefully as the door swung open and Maria came in with the white kitten cuddled in her arms.

"Here we are. Now, like I said, she's very friendly but she's still quite little, so be gentle." Maria sat down on the floor with the white kitten standing on her lap. "There you go, little one," she murmured. "You go and have a look around." Then she smiled at Abi and her family. "I know she can't hear me, but I keep forgetting and I talk to her anyway!"

The white kitten stood there, looking around curiously. She's so pretty, Abi thought. Even prettier close up, when you could see how blue her eyes were and the shell-pink of her nose and ears. Even her tiny paws were pinkish.

"So does being deaf make a big difference to how we look after her?" Chris asked.

"Well, you won't be able to call her and she won't hear food going into her bowl or anything like that. But she can definitely pick up vibrations." Maria slapped her hand on the floor and the kitten looked round curiously. "You see? It's not the noise she's responding to, it's the feel – the vibrations in the air. You can teach her to use hand signals too, like beckoning her to come to you, or maybe touching your mouth to say it's food time. I've got a handout to give you with some ideas."

"You mean, we can train her?" Abi asked. "Like a dog?" She slipped down off her chair to sit on the floor with Maria, and the white kitten watched her.

"Sure. Cats are really clever. And most cats will do anything for food. If she comes when you beckon and you give her a nice treat, she's going to learn it's a good thing to do."

"Oh, she *is* coming to me," Abi whispered as the white kitten padded across the floor. "Hello, kitten." Then she looked up at Maria. "It seems weird not to talk to her."

"I know what you mean. And of course you still can – just as long as you don't get cross when she doesn't notice. Actually, if you talk, she might understand your body language. Go big on the facial expressions," Maria suggested. "Big smiles if you're pleased with her and frown if she's jumped up somewhere she shouldn't."

"Is it OK for Abi to stroke her?" Mum asked, and Ruby reached towards the kitten. "Me too!"

"Your turn in a minute, Ruby," Chris said.

"It's fine to stroke her – but just tap your fingers on the floor in front of her first, Abi, so you don't give her a shock. She's looking at you right now anyway but it's a good idea to get into the habit of showing her you're there."

Abi tapped her nails on the floor and the kitten put her head to one side, obviously intrigued. She sniffed Abi's fingers, and stood still while Abi gently stroked her little pink ears. Then she began to purr, a huge clickety purr that made Abi laugh.

"She's so noisy!"

"Yes, that's another thing about deaf cats – she can't hear how loud she's being. And it might be that she enjoys the feel of making a noise. She's got a really loud meow as well."

"Ruby, do you want to stroke her?" Abi suggested. "She's so soft."

Ruby nodded eagerly and scrambled down from Mum's knee. "Shall I tap?" she asked Maria seriously, and Maria smiled at her. "Yes, that would be great. Well done."

The white kitten looked round as Ruby banged the floor and Ruby gazed silently back at her. Abi couldn't believe how good her little sister was being – it was almost as if the kitten had made her shy. Ruby reached out her hand slowly and the kitten padded forward and licked her fingers.

"Her tongue's all rough!" Ruby whispered. Then she looked round at Mum and Chris. "When are we taking her home?"

Chapter Four

Abi had hoped they might be able to take the white kitten home straight away, once Mum and Chris had signed all the paperwork and paid her adoption fee. But they weren't going to be allowed to have her until the weekend. There was a lot to do first, Chris pointed out as they were driving home. "We need to get her a basket –

maybe one of those igloo ones. Litter trays, food bowls, toys. A scratching post."

"Yes, and we need to walk round the house and think about what we need to do. Maria's going to come back for a visit in a day or two, to help us get ready for an indoor kitten," Mum said, turning round to look at Ruby and Abi in the back of the car.

Abi sighed. "Does that mean we have to tidy up again?"

Chris snorted with laughter. "Actually, Maria gave me a leaflet to read about indoor cats while your mum was signing papers. It says that they like a nice cluttered space with lots of stuff to hide behind. So our house should be perfect."

"Can I have a look?" Abi asked, and Mum found the leaflet and passed it back to her. Abi glanced through it. "Wow. There's a lot to learn, isn't there? I didn't know we had to give the kitten grass."

"What?" Chris sounded surprised. "I missed that bit. Grass, really?"

"Yes. It says here that it helps them get the hair out of their stomachs. Why would they have hair in their stomachs though? Oh, I suppose it's because they're always licking themselves. We have to have a little pot of grass for her to nibble on!"

When they got back home, Abi finished reading the leaflet lying on her bed. There *was* a lot to do. Mum had already said they'd have to get some sort of screen to put over the windows – she hated the idea of keeping them all closed in the summer.

While Mum and Chris were making dinner, Abi sat at her desk and started making a list of everything they needed for their kitten. It was a long list but she didn't mind. Every little thing she wrote down seemed to make the kitten more theirs. And in a few days' time, they would be bringing her home.

The white kitten sniffed anxiously at the sides of the box and mewed. She didn't know what was happening but the last time she had been carried in a box she had been taken away from her mother. She had been well fed at the shelter and her brother and sister had been there to snuggle with, but it wasn't the same. With her mother she had been safe and warm…

The box tipped a little and the kitten slid into the corner with a frightened squeak. She crouched there, huddled and mewing for what seemed like hours as the box swayed and tipped and lurched. And then it stopped – she was on solid ground again, she could feel it. She sat up and glared as the flaps at the top were opened.

There were faces peering inside and she crouched back into her corner miserably. She was somewhere new, she could smell it.

"She doesn't look very happy," Abi said. "I wish we'd got her one of those special carriers with a wire front so she could see out."

"We will," Mum agreed. "It was just getting a bit expensive, everything all at once. So when Maria said we could have this carrying box, it seemed like a good idea. But you're right, she looks positively cross. Don't you, sweetheart?"

"Get her out," Ruby begged. "I want to cuddle her."

The kitten squeaked again as Mum reached in to lift her out. "I don't think she wants cuddling right now, Ruby.

She's a bit confused."

"Shall we just let her look at her new basket and toys?" Abi suggested. "I thought she'd be happy to have a proper home. But I don't think she understands that's what this is yet."

The kitten slunk across the floor, sniffed cautiously at the igloo basket and darted inside. Then she crouched down in the opening and peered out suspiciously at the family staring back at her.

Chris sighed but he was grinning, and Abi frowned at him. "What are you smiling like that for?"

"I don't know. I suppose I've just never seen a crosser-looking cat. She's so tiny and sweet but every hair of her is cross."

"Perhaps we should feed her," Mum suggested, and Abi hurried to fetch one of the new kitten food pouches they'd stocked up with.

The kitten twitched as she saw Abi gently tilting the food bowl towards her. She could smell the food – the same kind that she was used to. She was quite hungry… Slowly, she put her nose out of the basket and eyed the people crowded around. There were too many of them.

"She isn't just cross, she's scared," Abi said suddenly. "We should leave her alone."

"But I want to cuddle her!" Ruby said, looking upset.

"Me too." Abi sighed. "But we have to wait a bit. Look at her, Ruby. She's really frightened. She doesn't even want to come and eat her lunch."

"She's like you were, Ruby, on the first day of Reception," Mum pointed out. "Let's all give her some space."

Ruby sniffed. On her first day of school, she'd had to be bribed with the promise of a new pot of bubble mixture to stop holding on to Mum's legs, and she still had days where she didn't want to go into the classroom. She tiptoed away from the kitten and sat down on a kitchen chair to watch.

The kitten stepped carefully out
of the basket and went to the food
bowl. For a little while she was more
interested in the food than she was
worried about this strange new place.
But once the bowl was empty, she
looked around and they were all still
there, watching her.

The bigger girl was sitting on the
floor with a feather toy in her hand.
There had been one of those to play
with before. The kittens had loved it,
dancing and jumping and falling over
each other to catch the feathers and
twinkling ribbons.

The shiny ribbons caught the light
as the girl shook the toy. The kitten
padded closer, just to look. Then the

feathers twitched again and she bounced, all four paws off the ground, to catch them. One paw came close, her claws just skimming the edge of the feathers, but the toy jumped away. She crouched down to stalk it across the floor, waiting until the moment was just right. Then she sprang straight up and thumped it hard with her paw.

She landed half in Abi's lap, slipping down her knees. Abi put a hand out to catch her, gently scooping the kitten up.

Abi was still holding the stick for the cat toy and the bundle of feathers was dangling next to her now. The kitten sat up on her hind paws and grabbed it, hugging it tight. She settled back on Abi's lap to chew on the feathers and forgot that she was scared.

"We need to decide what to call her," Chris said, watching Ruby and Abi stroking the white kitten, who was stretched out between them on the sofa half asleep. They had danced the feather toy about for her all afternoon and she was worn out. She'd eaten another kitten food pouch and she'd worked out where her litter tray was.

She's doing amazingly, Abi thought. Especially since Maria had warned that it might take her days to settle in.

"It ought to be something to do with her colour," Mum suggested. "Or her blue eyes. We could call her Sapphire."

Abi made a face. "That's not very easy to say."

"Sky, then?"

Chris nodded. "That's better."

"My friend Sky would like that," Abi said, tickling the kitten under the chin.

"Oh, I'd forgotten… It might be a bit confusing though. What about Blanche? It's French for white."

Abi wrinkled her nose. "I don't think she looks like a Blanche. She's like – she's like…" Abi sighed. "I don't know! She's so pretty. And I love her pink nose – it's like a flower petal." She looked up at Mum and Chris suddenly. "We could call her Flower!"

Mum looked pleased. "That's a lovely name."

"Hey, Flower," Abi murmured as she stroked the white kitten again. The kitten didn't hear her, of course, but she began to purr, a purr so loud that Abi could feel Flower's whole furry little body shaking under her fingers.

On Sunday, Flower began to explore her way all through the house. It took her a while to get upstairs, as her legs were still a bit short for the steps, but

she was determined and Ruby gave
her a lift the last few steps to the top.
She sat on Ruby's bed and watched her
play and then tried to climb inside the
dolls' house. Then she slept on Abi's
lap while she did her homework.

Sometimes she sat on the back of
the sofa and watched the road outside
through the front window, but she
didn't seem to mind that she was
an inside cat. She didn't know any
different, Abi decided. Actually, even
if they'd adopted a kitten who *wasn't*
deaf, it would have had to stay inside
for a while, Maria had told them.
Kittens couldn't go out until they'd had
all their vaccinations.

The leaflet had been right when it
said that indoor cats liked things to

hide behind. Flower went under the sofa, inside the pan cupboard and nearly got stuck behind the bookcase in the living room. She loved climbing too.

On Monday morning before school, Abi came into the kitchen to get her cereal and looked around to see where Flower was. She'd hurried down before she got dressed and found the kitten still curled up asleep in her igloo basket – but she definitely wasn't there now. It was only when she heard a tiny meow that she realized where Flower was. She was perched on the curtain rail over the kitchen window and she looked a bit worried.

"Mum!" Abi yelled. "You need to come and see this!"

Flower mewed again and tried to
stand up, slipping a bit.

"How did she get up there?" Mum
said, stopping in the doorway to stare.

"I don't know, but I think she's about
to fall off! Can you reach her?"

Mum unhooked the kitten and
made a frowny face at her, wagging her
finger like a cross mother in a cartoon.

"What are you doing?" Abi asked
her mum. Then she giggled, watching

Flower stalk across the kitchen floor to her water bowl, pretending she hadn't been stuck at all.

Mum laughed too. "I was trying to do a big facial expression, like Maria said. So she understood I was cross."

"Ohhh. I'm not sure it was her fault though. I was reading about deaf cats on the internet and one of the websites said they liked being high up because it makes them feel safe. Like no one could creep up on them."

"Maybe. But she can't get into the habit of climbing the curtains," Mum said firmly. Then she turned, looking towards the front door. "Oh no, is that the dustmen? I haven't put the bin out!" She hurried from the kitchen to open the front door. "Abi, make sure you're holding Flower or watching that she doesn't go out."

Abi crouched down by the kitten but Flower hadn't even noticed that the front door was open. Abi heard the door close and went to get her cereal. Flower finished her drink and padded out into the hallway.

"I nearly missed them!" Mum said, coming back with a relieved look on her face. Then her eyes met Abi's and they both whirled round at the sound of the front door clicking open.

"It's the bin lorry!" Ruby cried excitedly, waving to the man pulling the dustbin away from the front gate. "Hello! Hello!"

The bin man waved back and Ruby jumped up and down happily. Behind her, a curious white kitten hurried towards the door and Abi raced up the hallway.

"Ruby, don't let her out!"

Ruby turned round, surprised and then horrified, as Flower slipped past her feet. Abi lunged forward, grabbing the white kitten just before she shot out of the door.

"Oh Abi, well done!" Mum gasped, hurrying down the hall after her. "That was close!"

Chapter Five

"I'd have been so cross with her,"
Sky said when Abi told her about it
later on.

"I was a bit – but Ruby's only little
and she was really upset when Mum
explained what she'd done wrong."
Abi shook her head. "It's so tricky!
I never thought we opened the front
door that much. But we do, loads.

And in the summer we leave the back door to the garden open all the time. Or we did."

Sky made a face. "Are you thinking an indoor cat's going to be too much trouble?"

"No way! We'll just have to be careful. Flower's so gorgeous. She's still a bit shy sometimes, but we've only had her for a few days. I *think* she likes us."

"Of course she likes you," Sky said encouragingly. "Or she should do. It sounds like you're being perfect indoor cat owners."

They were trying, anyway – but it was a lot more work than anyone had expected, even after all they'd done to get ready. After Flower had climbed the curtains for the third time, Mum and Chris decided she needed something of her own to climb. So on Saturday they went to the pet shop to choose her a cat tree – a sort of special climbing frame for a cat with scratching posts, a box to hide in and a little hammock to sleep in.

Flower loved it and the hammock was her new favourite sleeping place, much better than her basket.

She lolled about in it with her paws in the air and her chin hanging over the edge so she could see what was going on.

Abi wasn't sure if Flower was so nosy because of her deafness or if all cats were like that, but the little kitten hated to miss anything. She had to climb and sniff and probably scratch everything that came in the house. She loved Abi and Ruby's room because it was full of toys and blankets and things to explore and snuggle under. Sometimes she slept on Abi's bed, but Mum always came and got her before she and Chris went to bed. Mum wasn't sure that Flower would be able to make it down the stairs when she needed the litter tray.

Halfway through Flower's second

week with the family, Ruby brought home a junk model from school. Junk modelling was her favourite thing about Reception but Mum had made a rule – one model in, one model out. Otherwise Abi and Ruby's room would be completely full of cereal packets stuck to toilet-roll tubes.

The new model was a cat – actually it was Flower, or so Ruby said. Abi couldn't quite see it, only that there were some soggy bits of white tissue paper stuck on.

"Flower knows it's her," Ruby said proudly, setting it down on the floor in front of the kitten and watching as she sniffed it and then tried to climb inside the tissue box that was her body.

"You know what," Abi said

thoughtfully, "there was something like that on one of the websites I was looking at about indoor cats."

Chris looked at her in surprise. "What, making junk models for them to shred? Ruby, if you don't want her to eat it, I'd go and put it somewhere high up in your bedroom."

"Not to claw at. To get food out of." Abi frowned, trying to remember. "It said that outdoor cats spend ages tracking and hunting, and even if they never actually catch anything it's good for indoor cats to have something like that too. That you should make their food into a puzzle. There was a picture that looked just like one of Ruby's models. It was all loo rolls stuck together, and there were cat biscuits hidden inside it. Like the biscuits Flower sometimes has for her tea now."

"That's a great idea." Chris reached out to the back of the kitchen door, where there was a cloth bag hung on a hook. "There you go. We were saving these for Ruby to take into school. *Loads* of loo rolls."

"Can I help?" Ruby asked, cuddling her junk cat protectively while Flower pranced around her ankles, purring with excitement.

The pyramid of loo roll tubes was so huge it took ages for all the glue to dry. Abi and Ruby had made it very carefully. They cut extra holes in some of the tubes and blocked other ones off half way with milk-bottle tops so that it was like a kitten intelligence test. When it was finally dry enough to let Flower anywhere near, it became her new favourite toy.

She was asleep in her hammock when Abi gently shook the box of special dry kitten food close by and then tapped her fingers on the box. Flower's eyes snapped open, bright blue against her white fur, and her ears twitched. Even though she couldn't hear, Flower still used her ears for signalling. They twitched *a lot*.

She hopped down the levels of her cat tree and hurried into the kitchen to her food bowl, which was empty. She sniffed at it, confused, and then turned round to stare accusingly at Abi. They had shaken the food box at her – Abi had touched her hand to her mouth too, the way she always did when there was going to be food. But there wasn't any.

Abi was tapping her fingers on the floor though, and Flower could still smell cat biscuits. She sniffed curiously at the pile of cardboard tubes that Abi and Ruby had set down in front of them. That was where the smell was coming from, she was almost sure. She peered in. Yes, there was definitely a cat biscuit inside, but the tube was just a little too narrow to get her head in. She mewed and Ruby reached for the biscuit.

"No, don't get it for her," Abi said. "She needs to work it out."

With a confused little hiss, Flower
stretched up, so she could reach in
with one small paw. She scrabbled
about a bit and then hooked out the
biscuit, sending it bouncing on to
the floor. Then she gobbled it up
triumphantly.

"You see!" Abi yelped, high-fiving
Ruby. "I told you she'd do it!"

"She's finding more," Ruby said,
giggling as Flower nearly tipped over
the pyramid by standing right up on

her hind legs to claw out a biscuit from the top. "She likes it!"

The cat tree and the food-hunting pyramid were meant to help keep Flower busy inside, so she didn't feel stressed because she couldn't go outdoors. They worked – but not completely. The kitten still loved to sit on the back of the sofa and watch the comings and goings in the street. She was fascinated by cars driving up and down the road – Abi could see her following them, turning her head as they sped by.

She still wanted to see what was going on every time they went to the front door too. She couldn't *hear* the bell but Abi thought she could maybe *feel* it – their doorbell was quite loud and sharp. Flower always seemed to come running when it rang, unless she was upstairs.

Abi and Ruby had to pick her up every time the door was answered or she'd be trying to slip round Mum or Chris's feet. Flower would wriggle eagerly in their arms, her whiskers twitching as she sniffed all those outdoor smells.

After the bin men, there were a couple of other near misses where Flower was just so wriggly that Abi couldn't hold on to her. Chris had to shut the door quite suddenly on the postman to stop the little kitten dashing out.

That night at dinner he told Mum

and Abi and Ruby that he was thinking of building Flower a catio – a cat patio out in the garden with wire sides and a roof so she could sunbathe and explore outdoors.

Abi giggled and looked down at Flower, who was sitting on her lap, hoping Abi would drop bits of sausage. "I bet she'll still try and get out of the front door."

"Of course she will." Chris rolled his eyes. "But it's better than nothing. She obviously really likes the idea of being outside."

A couple of days after her near escape past the postman, Flower was dozing in her hammock, softly flexing her tiny claws in and out as she dreamed. She blinked and squeaked to herself, and half woke up as she felt Chris's heavy footsteps going past the living room, where the cat tree was. She popped her head out, watching him walk into the kitchen, and wondered what he was doing. It didn't *feel* as if it was food time, but it might be…

She wriggled out of her hammock and hopped down on to the floor, meaning to follow Chris. Then she noticed the shopping bags that he'd left in the hallway. They were just by the living-room door – one big bag full of books and a couple of empty ones. They looked interesting.

She sniffed at them – so many smells!

Food smells and people smells and others she had no idea about… Flower scrabbled her way up the side of the largest bag, trying to investigate – and then she realized that she could get inside. The bag of books smelled strange, but the plasticky stuff they were covered in was good for her claws. She flexed them in and out happily.

Then the footsteps thumped back and the bags swayed and lifted. There was a rush of cool air.

Flower didn't know it, but she was outside at last.

Chapter Six

"Chris – hi!"

The library books shifted under Flower's paws as Chris set the bag down and started chatting to the neighbour who'd waved at him. The bag slumped open, revealing the pile of books and the little white kitten perched between them. Flower peered over the edge of the bag and then hopped out. Chris and the neighbour were too busy gossiping and complaining about someone dumping an old mattress on the grass verge down the road to notice her. Flower padded away, sniffing thoughtfully at the cars-and-lorries smell of the air.

She wandered along the pavement, flinching at the rumble of the cars' wheels and the way the air moved as they sped by her. It ruffled her fur and her whiskers, and she knew that they were large and perhaps dangerous. A big truck went past, scaring her with its heavy rattling vibration and Flower crouched down by a gatepost, where it felt a little safer.

Then
there was
a sudden
rush of air
and movement
as a car rolled past her
into the driveway, so close
that the ground shook under her paws
and her ears and whiskers were blown
straight back.

The kitten stumbled backwards with
a mew of fright. She had never seen a
car so close up – she didn't know what
was happening.

The car's engine was turned off and
the terrifying shake of the ground
settled to an uneasy nothing. Flower
stayed frozen for a couple of seconds
and then raced away, desperate to

escape the fearful rumbling thing that she was sure had almost flattened her. She dashed wildly along the pavement, shooting round a corner into a side road and then down a little alley.

The shuddering vibrations of the cars were a little further away now and her hammering heart slowed. She flung herself under a clump of scruffy bushes and crouched there among the dead leaves and dust, shivering each time another car shook the ground.

Mum didn't have any meetings after school that day so she brought Abi and Ruby home, rather than Chris picking them up as he usually did. They opened the front door in the careful, kitten-watching way they'd learned, peering round to make sure that Flower was nowhere nearby, and then bundling themselves in.

But Flower wasn't anywhere to be found. They searched and searched, all over the house, in every cupboard and on top of every bookcase, in all the places they'd ever found her lurking.

"Perhaps she's asleep and can't hear us…" Abi said, even though she knew that couldn't be true. Somehow Flower always knew when they were home. She would appear, padding eagerly down the hall and rubbing herself round their ankles until someone picked her up.

"Maybe she's got out," Mum said worriedly, looking about as though she expected to see an open window.

"She can't have done." Chris shook his head. "I checked before I went to the library and the shops. She was asleep in her cat tree – and even if she hadn't been, I'd have noticed her sneaking out of the door. She's got to be here somewhere. She just has to."

But she wasn't, even though they searched everywhere all over again, with Ruby crying and Abi trying very hard not to. At last even Chris had to admit that Flower wasn't anywhere to be found. "We'd better go and look for her outside," he said, sounding shaken.

"What if she's gone in the road?" Abi whispered. She was thinking about what Maria had said – that the road in front of their house was too dangerous for a cat. Any cat, let alone a kitten who couldn't hear and had never been outside before. Not since she was really tiny and been found in a box, anyway.

Mum swallowed. "I'm sure she wouldn't… She'd be scared. I expect she's hiding in someone's garden. We'll go and look."

They went outside, peering around the front garden, looking under all the bushes and over the fence into next-door.

"Flower! Flower!" Ruby called, and Abi glared at her.

"She can't hear you, Ruby! Don't be silly!"

Ruby sniffed loudly and began to cry again. "Abi's being horrible to me!"

"You're right, Abi, but you shouldn't shout at Ruby like that," Mum told her. "Actually, I wonder if there *is* a way we can call her? Tapping isn't going to work, not unless she's really close."

"I don't think so. There's too much noise and vibration from the road." Chris shook his head. "And I still don't understand how she could have got out. I'm going to walk down the street and look in all the gardens. Do you want to come with me, Abi?"

"Yes." Abi nodded. She was so worried and upset that it was making her grumpy, and if she stayed searching their garden she'd probably snap at Ruby again.

They walked out on to the pavement just as a car raced past and Abi shivered. She tried to imagine what it would have felt like to Flower if she'd come out on to the pavement – the kitten would have been terrified. Abi leaned over the fence, trying to see round the bushes in next-door's garden, while Chris did the same in the garden along.

"Are you all right?"

Abi looked up in surprise. She hadn't noticed their neighbour, Annika, opening her front door. "We've lost our kitten," she explained. "Sorry about leaning over your fence – I was looking for her. She's meant to be an indoor cat, you see. She's deaf."

"Oh no – well you're very welcome to come into the garden and see if you can find her." Annika stepped out on to her front path and crouched down to look around. "What colour is she?"

"She's white and she's really tiny."

Annika looked up, her eyes widening. "A really little white cat? I think I saw her this afternoon!"

"You did?" Abi felt her hands tighten on top of the fence. "Where was she?"

"Running down the pavement. She was further along the road, a few houses down from the supermarket." Annika frowned. "And she was definitely going that way."

Abi stared at her. The supermarket was right at the end of the road. She had been hoping that Flower would be in Annika's garden or possibly the next one along. How could Flower have gone so far? She must have been terrified, with all the cars speeding by on the busy road. "Wh-when was that?" she asked, her voice shaking a little.

"Well, my shift finished at two," Annika said. "So it must have been about half past, I guess." She looked worriedly at Abi. "It might not have been her…" she added gently.

"Did she have blue eyes?" Abi asked, not sure whether to hope Annika would say yes or no.

"I *think* so… She was running, I didn't see her for very long…"

"Thanks – I'd better tell Chris." Abi turned to look for her stepdad but he was already walking back towards them.

"Did Abi explain, Annika? About our cat?" Chris asked.

"Annika saw her!" Abi burst out. "All the way down the road, going towards the supermarket!"

Chris turned round to look, and Abi

saw him make a face without meaning
to. He was thinking what she was
thinking – that their road joined on to
another one close by the supermarket,
which was even busier. It definitely
wasn't somewhere a little deaf kitten
wanted to be running about.

"Thanks, Annika. You've been really
helpful." Chris nodded to her. "Sorry
to disturb you. We'll go and look down
there for her now."

Abi slipped her hand into his as they
walked along and Chris squeezed her
hand. "We'll find her, Abi," he said
firmly. "It's going to be OK."

Abi nodded. She wanted to think
so too. But as the cars kept rolling
by, she wasn't so sure that her stepdad
was right.

Chapter Seven

"There must be a better way of looking for her," Chris said, running his fingers through his hair and looking down the street. "This just isn't working."

They'd been out for over an hour now. Mum and Ruby had helped to start with but then Ruby got tired and upset and Mum had taken her home for a snack. Abi and Chris had kept on searching. Abi had even nipped back into the house for the tin they kept the kitten biscuits in, as she was sure Flower felt the vibrations when they shook them at home. There was probably too much going on for her to notice it out here but Abi was going to try everything.

"Mum could put a post about Flower on the school parents' online chat," Abi suggested. "The one where people ask about which day is swimming and what to bring for trips. Loads of people from school live on this road. Someone else might have seen her."

"That's a good idea," Chris agreed. "There are lost cat websites as well – we can add her to those. And if she's still missing tomorrow, we'll make some posters."

"Tomorrow?" Abi heard her voice go high and squeaky. She'd been sure that they would get Flower back that day. They had to. She couldn't imagine her tiny little kitten outside on her own all night.

"We need to go home and have something to eat, Abi," Chris said gently. "It's nearly six and we haven't spoken to anyone else who's seen her. We can come out again after that but it'll be getting dark soon."

"She'll be easy to see in the dark," Abi said stubbornly, thinking of Flower's pure-white fur.

"I know — it's just so hard when we can't call for her." Chris looked around, frustrated. "She could be right here, waiting for us to find her."

"Don't say that!"

"Sorry." He gave Abi a hug. "Come on. Let's go and get some dinner. Mum sent me a text to say it's ready."

"OK. But I'm coming out to look again afterwards."

Chris nodded. "We will."

In the end, Ruby wanted Chris to read her a bedtime story and she was so miserable about Flower being missing that it was easier not to argue with her. So after Abi nibbled a bit of pasta, Mum went out with her to look again instead. She got a torch from the kitchen drawer because it was just starting to get dark.

They walked down the street,

stopping to tap on gateposts and stamp their feet outside each garden. But no little white shape dashed out to meet them and Abi's heart seemed to sink a little bit more with every house they passed. It was sitting somewhere on top of her stomach now and she felt sick with worry.

"I wonder if we should call the shelter," Mum said as they reached the supermarket at the end of the road. "Just in case someone's found Flower and handed her in."

"But then they'll know we didn't look after her properly," Abi whispered.

"Oh Abi, love. I'm sure they won't think that. We've done everything they said…"

"Except we let her out!" Abi gasped. She'd been trying so hard not to cry all this time, but now she couldn't help it. "What if she gets run over? What if she already has been? They said it's happened on this road before…"

"Someone would have seen and told us," Mum said firmly. "And I think the shelter will be closed now anyway. So we can't ring them tonight. But I think we'll have to tomorrow morning, if we haven't found her by then."

Flower stayed huddled under the bushes. She had peeped out into the darkening alley a few times, but she could still see the blurred lines of cars shooting along the road at the end, and she remembered how one of them had come so close to her. She didn't understand why that had happened, but she dreaded that rumbling rush and the blast of air through her

whiskers. The
bushes were safe,
even if her fur
was smeared
with dust.
Yes, she
could just
stay here…

But if she did
that, she wouldn't be able to get
home. Abi and Ruby would have put
food out for her to find, and she was
hungry. She had sniffed around in the
dead leaves for something to eat but
all she had found was a beetle that
was crunchy and tasted strange when
she'd tried to eat it. She was so, so
hungry. She wanted her food and to
have Ruby dance a toy about for her,

and then to be lifted up on Abi's lap to sleep.

She had to get home. Even if meant going back to that road again.

Abi lay in bed listening to Ruby's snuffled hiccupy breathing. Ruby had been crying again, and she'd woken up when Abi came to bed and crawled in with her. She'd cried all over Abi's pyjamas so Abi felt damp and even more miserable and she just couldn't sleep.

"Are you OK, Abi, love?" Mum whispered from the doorway. "Are you awake?"

"A little bit," Abi whispered back.

"We're going to bed now," Mum said, coming to crouch down by Abi's bed. "Do you want me to put Ruby back in her own bed?"

"No, she'll wake up. It's OK."

"I'm sure we'll find Flower tomorrow." Mum stroked her hair. "Chris will look for her while we're all at school."

"OK." Abi didn't know what else to say. She was sure she couldn't spend the day doing literacy and maths while Flower was still missing. But her mum was a teacher – she was never going to agree to let Abi have the day off school to keep on looking.

Mum shut the door gently and Abi wriggled a bit, trying to get comfortable next to Ruby. Her little

sister snuffled in her sleep and half
rolled over so that she was up against
the wall. She took most of the
duvet with her and Abi sighed and
pulled her old cuddly fleece blanket
up around her instead. It smelled
comforting, like washing powder,
and she snuggled it up by her face,
sniffing it sadly.

Then she stopped and sat up on her elbow, staring into the darkness.

Smell!

One of the websites she'd read had said deaf cats probably had better other senses than cats who could hear, because they depended on those senses more and practised using them. And Abi had definitely read somewhere else that one thing you could do for a lost cat was put their bed or their litter tray outside the house, because cats had brilliant noses and would smell their own scent and find their way home.

So Flower would be even better at that than an ordinary cat, wouldn't she?

Abi slid carefully out of bed, trying not to wake Ruby, and wrapped her blanket round her shoulders. She hesitated on the landing outside Mum and Chris's room – should she wake them? If she did, they'd probably go and put the litter tray outside and tell her to go back to bed.

But Abi wanted to be there – she wanted to watch, in case it worked. What if they put the litter tray outside and went back to bed, and then Flower came? She wouldn't understand why her litter tray was there and nobody was waiting for her. She might go away again.

So Abi tiptoed down the stairs and into the kitchen to fetch the litter tray. Luckily no one had cleaned it out – it didn't smell very much to Abi but she bet Flower would be able to smell it for miles. She hoped so anyway. This had to work. It had to.

She unlocked the front door carefully and couldn't stop herself glancing round to make sure Flower wasn't racing down the hallway to see what was happening. "Stupid," she muttered to herself. Then she slipped outside, shivering in the night air, and set the tray down on the path.

She stood in the gateway, looking up and down the road, hoping to see a little white shape hurrying towards her through the darkness but there was no one around. It was eerie.

Abi retreated back indoors so she could watch from the living-room window. She sat down on the sofa just next to where Flower liked to sit. Her eyes were adjusting to the darkness now and she was sure she could see a few of Flower's white hairs against the dark fabric. She knelt up, leaning her elbows on the back of the sofa, and stared determinedly out of the window.

She was going to stay awake until Flower came home.

Chapter Eight

Flower stepped out from underneath the bushes and looked down the alleyway. It was fully dark now and she'd been getting colder and colder huddled there. She felt stiff, and slow, and she wasn't sure she could run away if one of those rumbling things came near her again. But to get back home she supposed she would have to go along the road and risk it. She padded down the dark alley and then flinched as something ran in front of her. She had a moment's glimpse of white teeth gleaming and a massive paw swept the air in front of her nose, cuffing her and knocking her sideways. She jumped and twisted and rolled over, landing half on her side as the creature loomed over her. Then it darted away.

Flower lay crouched and gasping in the dust, making herself as small as she could, wondering if the creature was going to come back. What was it? Another cat? It must have been. The smell seemed right, but it had been so much larger than she was. She wasn't sure if she should stay still, or run, or try to hide. But the cat seemed to have moved on and even though there were scents of other animals around, there was nothing else nearby.

At last she began to move forward again, creeping cautiously along the alleyway to the road. And then she stopped, almost forgetting how much the larger cat had scared her. She had expected the road to be busy and frightening. She had been steeling herself for the speed of the cars and the way they made the air whoosh past her whiskers.

She hadn't expected to be lost.

Which way should she turn out of the alleyway? Which way was home? Which way back to Abi and Ruby? Flower felt the fur rising along her spine again and her tail fluffing up in panic. She was lost and there were more cats around – she could smell them. She was in their territory. Her territory was the house, and her basket, and the cat tree, and Abi. She was in the wrong place.

Flower hurried out of the alley and stood on the pavement, sniffing anxiously for the other cats' scent. She needed to get out of here. She had been lucky to be left alone all that time she was hidden under the bushes. But which way should she go now?

Her ears flattened against her skull as she realized that she needed to go towards the rumbling, shaking road, the busier road that she had run down. Home was that way, however much she hated the thought of it.

Whiskers bristling, she scurried down the street, darting along the innermost edge of the pavement in the shadow of the garden walls. When she came to the corner, she peered cautiously around at the cars speeding along the bigger road. Then she pressed herself against the wall with a mew of fright as a car turned into the side road towards her. But it rumbled on past without coming any closer.

Which way? Flower huddled against the wall, trying to stay calm and ignore the instinct inside that told her to just run and run, to get away from the cars. But that wasn't going to get her back to Abi and Ruby. After a few moments, she grew a little more used to the cars, and her fur began to lay flat again. She turned her head, trying to scent the way back home.

There was *something*... Flower grimaced, opening her mouth and curling her muzzle back over her teeth to smell better. She could smell *herself*. Her home – her territory. She bolted along the pavement, following the scent blowing on the wind. She was getting closer, the smell was stronger and she could feel it – she was nearly home.

At last – there it was! Her litter tray. But outside the house, not where it was meant to be. Flower padded into the front garden, sniffing at the litter tray cautiously. What was it doing out here? And how was she going to get into the house? She went over to sniff at the door – this was the way she had come out, carried in that bag. But now it was shut fast and it didn't move even when she scrabbled and mewed.

Flower sat down on the doorstep feeling cold and even hungrier now that she was so close to her food bowl. She mewed again, even louder, but still no one came.

Was there another way she could get in? Wearily, she turned and walked back down the path, looking at the big pot of flowers by the front door and the window up above. She knew that window – it was where she sat to watch the street and the people passing by. Except now she was on the other side, looking in…

She sprang up on to the edge of the flowerpot and made a scrabbly jump on to the windowsill. Then she peered through the glass. There was the sofa… Flower mewed loudly in frustration and then pressed her nose closer towards the glass.

Abi was there! She was asleep, her head pillowed on the back of the sofa, on the other side of the glass.

Flower stood up on her back paws, mewing and mewing, batting at the glass with her front ones. She could *see* Abi – so why wouldn't Abi wake up and notice her?

Abi was dreaming she was chasing down the road after her little white kitten, always just too far away to catch her before she disappeared. She was calling and calling, but all the time she knew it was useless – Flower couldn't hear her. It was heartbreaking. Flower was so frightened. Abi could hear her mewing in the dream and the noise was frantic. Flower was racing so fast that her paws were thudding on the ground…

Abi blinked and sat up a little, dazed with sleep. She had been dreaming that Flower was lost. No… She swallowed miserably. That wasn't a dream, her kitten really *was* lost.

She looked around, confused about where she was – and then she remembered. The litter tray outside. She had been trying to give Flower a scent to follow… Abi shook her head, trying to wake herself up properly. She hadn't meant to go to sleep and she could still hear the mewing from her dream. It was even getting louder and she could hear the thumping paws too…

"Flower?" Abi stared. Her kitten was there on the other side of the window, paws scrabbling eagerly, her mouth wide open in a mew.

Abi jumped off the sofa, trailing her blanket, and raced for the front door, fumbling with the locks. At last she pulled it open and Flower darted in, purring. She stood up, patting at Abi's knees with her little white paws until Abi picked her up and snuggled them both in the blanket.

Abi blinked as the landing light went on and the glow spread down the stairs.

"Mummy!" Ruby called from the top of the staircase. "Dad! Abi's found Flower!" She stumbled down to hug Abi and stroke Flower's nose.

"She came back," Abi told her little sister. "She's so clever – she followed her own smell. Oh, she must be hungry." She tapped her mouth – the food sign they always used to show Flower it was time for a meal – and the white kitten stared back at her seriously. Then she lifted her paw and tapped it against her own mouth.

"She did the sign!" Ruby gasped.

"She can't have done…" Abi looked at Flower and tapped her mouth again.

The kitten patted her own mouth with her paw and then wriggled out of Abi's arms. She jumped to the floor and dashed into the kitchen to stand by her food bowl.

Abi grabbed one of the pouches from the cupboard and emptied it into the bowl and the two girls crouched by the food to watch Flower eat. Abi could hear Mum and Chris coming downstairs, and then Ruby dash out to tell them about Flower signing back.

"I'm so glad you found your way home," she whispered to Flower as the kitten licked the last bits of food from round the edges of her bowl. "You're so clever. But please don't ever do that again. And we'll be so careful too."

Flower padded towards her and climbed up into Abi's lap, licking lazily at one paw and sweeping it around her whiskers. Then she looked up at Abi with her huge blue eyes and began to purr.

HOLLY WEBB

Holly Webb started out as a children's
book editor and wrote her first series for
the publisher she worked for. She has been
writing ever since, with over one hundred
books to her name. Holly lives in Berkshire,
with her husband and three children.
Holly's pet cats are always nosying around
when she is trying to type on her laptop.

For more information
about Holly Webb visit:

www.holly-webb.com